Alaska's Three Pigs

written by
ARLENE LAVERDE

illustrations by
MINDY DWYER

PAWS IV

PUBLISHED BY SASQUATCH BOOKS

Once upon a time, in the wilds of **Alaska**, there were **three little pigs**. Now, these little pigs had traveled a long way to build homesteads in Alaska's bush.

They each wanted to find a piece of land on which to live and grow big cabbages. They arrived on the frontier in summer, during the bright, warm days of the **Midnight Sun**, when the sun seems to shine all through the night.

"It's too nice and sunny to work," said the first

little pig. "Let's go camping instead!"

"Good idea!" said the second little pig. "I'll pack

marshmallows that we can toast!"

"And I'll bring my fishing rod to catch salmon

in the rivers," said the third little pig. So the

three little pigs spent the long days of summer

hiking, camping, and fishing.

But soon the first autumn frost came, and

the sun no longer stayed out all day and into the night.

The third little pig said to his brothers, "We've had a good time,

but now we must find land and build

our homes before winter comes."

The pigs put on their heavy, thick coats made of fur,

down, and wool and started out across the

frosty frontier.

When the pigs had traveled some distance, the first little pig said,

"I'm tired and have walked far enough. I'll stop here in this

grove of spruce trees." So he said good-bye to

his brothers, and they continued on their way.

The first little pig looked around and spied an old trapper's

cabin among the trees. There were chinks in the walls,

the roof was moldy, and the stove was dented. "Well,"

thought the pig, "it's not pretty or clean, but it's better than

having to build my own cabin!" So he dropped his bag inside,

grabbed his snowboard, and headed to Mount McKinley.

The other two little pigs soon stopped to rest as an early snow began to fall. The second little pig decided he had traveled far enough and declared, "I'm going to build my house here on the wide open tundra."

So he said good-bye to his brother, who continued on his way.

As the second little pig stood on his homestead, he felt big, fat snowflakes landing on his snout.

"Hmmm," thought the little pig. "It's snowing harder, and I don't want to get stuck without a roof over my head."

The little pig cut down some small willows growing alongside a nearby river. He loosely braided the branches to make walls and patched together grass and moss for a roof. After a short time, the little pig had finished his house. "Done!" he cried.

Then he grabbed his skis and went to join his brother.

The third little pig was a smart little pig. He wanted a

strong house before the full force of winter came to Alaska.

In winter, he knew, it would be dark most of the time, and he

wanted to be protected from the bitter cold and from

hungry wild animals

As he walked along, the third little pig suddenly felt a cool mountain

wind blow down from a glacier. "Aha!" he cried.

He took a shovel, a pickax, and a sled up

into the foothills and carved out block after block

of glacier ice. It was hard work. He had to load the blocks

onto his sled and haul them back to his homestead site. It took several

trips and many long hours before the little pig had enough

blocks to begin building his igloo.

He carefully stacked the blocks, one on top of the other,

and filled in all the cracks with snow. He then poured

water over the walls so that they would freeze solid.

When he finished, he had a strong, safe house made of ice.

Now, the third little pig loved the outdoors as much as his brothers did, but before he went to play he wanted to get ready for the cold night ahead. He gathered wood to build a fire. Then he shoveled snow into a big barrel to melt for fresh drinking water. Finally, the little pig hooked some dogs to his sled and rode off to meet his brothers.

The little pigs loved to play in the snow! Whoosh! The first little pig made big turns on his snowboard. "Yeehaw!" the second little pig yelled joyfully as he followed on his skis. "Bark, bark!" the third little pig's dog team barked happily as he mushed them all around.

But all this noisy fun woke up a *grizzly* *bear* who was hibernating in a nearby cave. The grizzly was not happy to be disturbed. He had been sleeping for several weeks and was very, very hungry. "Grrrr," the bear grumbled, and "Grrrr," the bear's stomach *rumbled*, and the sound echoed out of the cave.

The third little pig pulled his dogsled to a *stop* and listened.

He said to his brothers, "It's getting very dark and cold now.

I think we should go back to our safe new homes."

No sooner had the first little pig latched the

rusty lock on his cabin door than he heard a soft knock.

"Little pig, little pig, let me come in," said the hungry grizzly bear.

Although the little pig was lazy, he was not stupid. He knew that

if he opened the door, he would be the grizzly's dinner.

"Not by the hair on my chinny chin chin," answered the little pig.

"Then I'll huff and I'll puff and I'll blow your house in," said the bear.

Taking a big, deep breath, he huffed and he puffed

and he blew on the little pig's cabin.

The rotten wood of the old cabin toppled under

the bear's hot breath, leaving the first little pig shaking by his dented

stove. But as the hungry bear swiped his big paw at

the pig, his claw caught on an old teakettle! He started

banging his paw on the stove to get it off—

and the first little pig quickly ran to the second little pig's house.

But as soon as the brothers were safe behind the

willow door, they heard a sharp rap

"Little pigs, little pigs," growled the grizzly, "I want to make my dinner, so let me come in!" The two little pigs were trembling in the corner— and it wasn't from the cold. "Not by the hair on our chinny chin chins!" cried the pigs.

"Then I'll huff and I'll puff and I'll blow your house in," grunted the grizzly bear. And he huffed and he puffed, he puffed and he huffed. He blew so hard that the small willows whirled around like a blizzard! In the confusion, the little pigs escaped and raced to the third little pig's igloo.

The three little pigs quickly shut the ice door.

As soon as they did, they heard a loud **pounding**

"Little pigs, little pigs, let me come in!" bellowed the bear.

"Not by the hair on our chinny chin chins,"

answered the smart third little pig.

"Then I'll huff and I'll puff and I'll blow your house in!"

roared the grizzly bear. So he huffed and he puffed, and he puffed and

he huffed. And he blew and he blew until **icicles** hung

from the tip of his nose and his breath came out in great big clouds.

But the igloo was strong. It did not **tumble** down

around the little pigs. It didn't even budge.

The hungry grizzly did not give up. Digging his claws into

the ice walls, he started to climb up to the top of the igloo.

"He'll come through the smoke hole!" squealed the first little

pig. The second little pig covered his eyes. But the third little pig had a

plan. He took the barrel of melted snow and pushed it out the door.

When the grizzly bear reached the top of the igloo, he looked

down and saw the third little pig standing outside.

This was his chance!

He jumped and slid down the icy wall . . . and landed

right in the **barrel** of water!

As the grizzly tried to get out of the barrel, the cold, cold air

froze his wet fur solid. Then the three little pigs loaded the

bear onto their dogsled and pushed and pulled him back

to his cave where he belonged. And where he would

not thaw out for a **very long time!**

The  End

Printed in China
08 07 06 05   9 8 7 6

Library of Congress Cataloging in Publication Data
Laverde, Arlene.
    Alaska's three pigs / text by Arlene Laverde; illustrations by Mindy Dwyer.
        p.   cm.
    Summary: Three pig brothers go to Alaska to build themselves new homes—with familiar
results.
    ISBN 1-57061-229-3 (alk. paper)
    ISBN 1-57061-272-2 (hardcover)
    [1. Folklore. 2. Pigs—Folklore.] I. Dwyer, Mindy, 1957– ill. II. Three little pigs. III. Title.
    PZ8.1.L342 A1 2000
    398.2'09798'04529633—dc21   00-029664

SASQUATCH BOOKS / 119 S. Main St., Suite 400 / Seattle, Washington 98104
800-775-0817 / custserv@SasquatchBooks.com / www.SasquatchBooks.com

To my family for their love and support.

And to the children of P.S. 92 for their inspiration.

—A.L.

For Sean, our littlest Alaskan.

—M.D.